HAN M GREENBARG

# Ember Dice

# Contents

# 1

# 2089



RUSSELL

Morgantown, West Virginia. Thursday. Hour: 1700.

"Scotch on the rocks."

"Ah. Diluting the burn today are we, Mr. Watke?"

"No, Ark. Just feeling happy."

"Happy is a wasted state on you. You always smilin' like an idiot."

"Gonna meet a girl."

The clink of ice knocking in the glass halted Ark mid-pour as he looked up. "Twenty-nine. At the end of the game, son."

"Eh," Russ said. "We'll see."

"You putting a ring on this one?"

"No ring."

Ark paced down the empty bar flicking a damp rag over the counter. "Gallon of broken hearts, Mr. Watke. What else you live on?"

"And the infamous Gerald Ark." Russ sipped and grinned as Ark glared at him. "You spent your years playing Ember Dice same as me. Now you at forty-two. No wife. No kids. Was it worth it?"

"Killing your own team is never worth it," he said. "And neither is destroying every girl you meet."

"Ah, c'mon, Ark. They love me. Public records show me as an eligible bachelor."

"Eligible in whose eyes?"

"And," Russ added with a wink, "I own the company."

Ark guffawed as he took his own swallow of top shelf rum. "Your uncle owns it. You ain't even in it by blood. Your mother's step-brother. And you walk free with no cries of injustice. Poor ladies. Not to mention you are the worst dresser I've met. That hoodie is the most decrepit yet."

"Yea man, screw it." He shrugged. "Dark horses are favored."

"Dark horse, my ass. You are the decorated soldier. The favorite. The world knows everything about you no matter what game you play."

"And that is what keeps me alive." Russ smiled at Ark. "Rolling warrior every time."

VIOLET

Ocean City, Maryland. Hour: 1800.

"Isn't it weird they don't allow photos on Ember Dice? How are we supposed to know if they are hot or not?"

"Trying to make us base it all on conversation. Less judgmental of the first look I guess. I mean, I had some nice emails with Russ so far."

"Yeah. My guy sounds nice on paper. His jokes are bad though."

"I need a good laugh," Violet said, kicking a pebble off the concrete path onto the sand.

"You design logos for the shuttle companies, right?" Megg, a fellow Ember Dice participant, walked next to her. She seemed to be silently judging Violet's battered sneakers against her own shimmering platform heels.

"I work for the last airline in our country. I write jingles that play overhead in the terminals."

"That line of work is gonna tank soon, girl."

"Yeah, seriously. Russ says he's ready to settle with a wife and I sure hope it's me."

"Well," Megg twittered with a perky bounce of her chest, "I just wanna see my guy's face finally. If he is goose ugly I'm ditching."

"You'd give up the free trip to Sciorlla? I'm sticking it out no matter what Russ looks like. I never get to travel anywhere."

"Maybe he can help you get a different job. A relevant one."

"Sure, maybe."

"Because it's your last chance, right? You're almost thirty. I'm only twenty-two. You don't match up on this trip and you'll be locked out of the site for good."

"I'm trying to be optimistic, Megg. We all get a guy."

"Yeah, but not all of us girls get hot ones. It's fair game to tag someone else."

"If the rules state we are allowed to switch partners I'm not going through with it," Violet said.

"Fine. I'll keep my guy whoever he is."

"What's his name again?"

"Firewall."

"Sounds like a cute jerk or conceited man-child."

"If he's hot I'd deal with the jerky aspect. He could look like a gargoyle. Or one of those guys whose fat is all stored up in their ass."

"I'm trusting the canon, Megg."

"What's the canon?"

"That's the site's version of an algorithm. Using ones and zeros and upside-down consonants to see who pairs up with who."

"Girl, that makes no sense."

"I never said I'm an expert on dating sites or how they work. I only paid for this after several of my friends found their loves that way. They begged me to give the site a shot."

"I just want a sexy nerd who's ready for kids."

"I think they are all nerds."

"Yes. We are."


COMMANDER RENT

"What time is it?"

"Six."

"AM or PM?"

"PM. When did you last look out the window, Wes?"

"Nothing but the dark void out there, sir. One more level then I'll have my pizza slice."

"Too bad. I already ate it."

Wesson glowered as Rent crossed in front of the screen with a shrug.

"The new recruits should be arriving just before sunrise," Rent said. "Has the base camp been checked?"

"It's ready for them, Commander."

Rent looked out at the swirls of constellations glowing up the pitch black of deep space.

"I wonder who Russ is going to bring," he murmured.

"It's his last year, isn't it?"

Their voices echoed in the ship's empty core. "He better not waste this one."

# 2

# Matches

VIOLET

Ember Dice Headquarters. Hour: 1900.

Violet thought it bizarre that out of the entire flock of dolled-up nerdy chicks there wasn't a single one openly giggling and twittering about her prospective mate and how hot she hoped he'd be. After finding out through the grapevine that she was the oldest participant among the women at twenty-nine years old, the anxiety from her wallflower high school days came flying back.

"Welcome, ladies. My name is Ellk. I am the owner of Ember Dice." The man strode down off the stage that was center in the banquet hall. He had a rigid posture, much like how virtual bamboo bends in a Southern Hemisphere breeze. "Each table you see here is for you and your match to begin the initial real world connection. Please take a seat where the card says your name and the gentlemen should be arriving within five minutes."

The eighteen young women fanned out among the tables, looking for their names, every single one being their gamer tag. Violet sat at her table and stared at the chair across from her.

"Where do you think the boys are at?" a bold drawling voice asked.

Violet glanced at the table next to her and down at the name on the card. Aura. Twenty-four years old.

"I assume they're allowed to be late," Violet said. "You know how guys are at this age. Little respect for the clock."

"You'd think geeks would appreciate time limits. Although when I messaged my Rivet in the first two weeks, he never knew when to sign off and let me go to bed. Speaking of age, Violet, you don't look twenty-nine. I swear you're only like twenty."

"Just good genes I guess." Violet watched Aura dig in her silver, sparkly purse and dump a fistful of eyeliners and lipsticks onto the table. She looked like a former cheerleader.

"I just don't like wearing makeup," Violet said. "Never have."

Aura gave a smile, more of a forced sympathy than an understanding vibe, as she applied a shade of maroon lipstick. "Different priorities, girl."

The faint sound of a 1980's tune drifted through the walls and twenty-one year old Corral had to state the obvious. "Where's that music coming from?"

Violet heard Aura whisper next to her. "I bet it's Russ."

RUSSELL

The guys had barely met fifteen minutes ago outside and formed an impromptu dance troupe as they did every year. They imbued the magic in his signature dance anthem as Russ led them through the entrance of Ember Dice Headquarters for the last time. He was a dark legend among the guys, and among the ladies he was an absolute celebrity.

"Russell Watke!" Ellk called out from the stage. "Take your

bow and turn that machine off. Please find your matches, gentlemen, before this night grows any longer."

Russ spun around like a superstar one more time and motioned his best friend to come forward. "Tuff, did I overdo it on the air guitar?"

"You get away with wearing a bland sweatshirt and jeans every year and somehow you always pull off this stupid dance. Why do we have to dress up like ritzy doormen?"

"I didn't tell you to look fancy tonight. I don't know any of these guys well enough except for you, Tuff. I told you to go casual this time."

"I got cut the first week because she hated my soap. She said it smelled like hay and turds."

"Hey." Russ yanked him by the collar of his shirt as the rest of the guys moved forward to meet their matches. "I warned you about the exotic scents way before you even signed up. Ember Dice girls don't like it. What's the magnet?"

"Pine and teakwood," Tuff mumbled.

"Yeah. Pine and teakwood. I hope you brought some this time." Russ shook his head as he watched Tuff shuffle toward the girls. He was the expert on winning over a woman in Ember Dice and if no one followed his advice it was their loss.

He only looked around at a few pretty females before he spotted Violet. She looked nothing like the other females but there was an unassuming flame in her humble form. Same age as him and both hoping for a true love connection. Russ put on a half-smile and made his move as he had done every time before.

VIOLET

Russ looked so much cuter than she had expected and the smile he gave to her as he approached was terrifying and heart-melting. She tried to fight off the swarm of butterflies that she hadn't felt since the days of her high school crushes. She tried to appear completely in control.

"Cricket," he said, using the pet name he had given her a few weeks into online messaging.

She held her breath when he dropped down to one knee. Every voice in the room paused and without glancing around Violet felt everyone watching them. The box he opened held a pendant on a chain.

"Will you be my Bullet Mate?"

Gasps, giggles, and rising whispers surrounded them in a fog.

"You're not serious, Russ," Violet whispered.

His smile widened. "Just say yes." There was a tinge of emotion, of choking-up in his voice. "You can trust me, Cricket."

"Yes." She blushed at the corny-sounding whistles and shrieks from the other participants.

Russ unhooked the chain and delicately put it around her neck, Violet lifting her long hair as he clasped it in the back and kissed her cheek.

"Talk about a smooth-talker," she said.

"I've done this a few times," he said with a wink. He sat down in the seat across from her and reached for her hands.

Few couples in the hall were shy with their initial affections. A month of chatting online was apparently plenty to get to know a guy. Violet laid her hands in his, letting the wild hormones course through.

"I feel like a high schooler again."

Russ laughed loudly. "You look it too."


RUSSELL

Ellk raised his hands and gave a sharp whistle. Everyone

looked in his direction as he began his standard greeting.

"Ladies and gentlemen, if you think this opportunity is just about a video game you are wrong. Bullet Rain will test every part of your strength, inner and outer. It is a mix of medieval and modern tech, barbaric methods and highly advanced strategies. In the end, this opportunity is not just about finding your dream lifemate. It is about survival. This is not Earth's game. Once you all board the transports and land on Sciorlla, you will belong to that planet's rules. There is nothing easy about this game and there is nothing easy about this journey. You will be risking your very lives in the hope that one couple out of dozens will win everything. If any person wishes to bow out of this opportunity, now is your last chance."

Several minutes of silence weaved through the tables before there was a small exodus out the front door. Ellk gave a quick look around.

"Twenty-eight? Look at that, they left us with an even number. Maybe they'll match themselves up in the bar next door."

A few people giggled at the comment while Russ rolled his eyes.

"Commander Piper, would you care to take over?" Ellk gestured to a stringy fellow dressed in an oceanic blue uniform. "These are your contenders."

Piper's wide grin was as playful as the gleeful green in his eyes. Age was heavy in his face and grey-streaked hair, but he spoke with the unhindered enthusiasm of a six-year-old boy, and he had a bounce in his step as he paced.

"I'm always tempted to call you cadets but in following protocol for the game we must go by your assigned positions. Have you tossed the dice yet?"

"No, Piper. I'm letting you facilitate that this time."

Russ leaned in over the table, ignoring Violet and the whispers around him to catch what he saw Ellk mouthing to Piper.

"This is our last one. Make it memorable." They both turned and saw Russ staring intently back. Piper shook his head at him and Ellk gave him a thumbs-up.

Russ gave a thumbs-up back. This was his year.


VIOLET

The tables and chairs were removed to create an open carpet space for the tossing of the dice. Each couple took a turn kneeling across from each other as the rest excitedly watched, one die given to the guy, one die given to the girl. Three sides of the die had a shield, the other three had a sword.

"It's rigged," Aura had warned her. "Us girls get the shield every time."

Russ tossed first, the die rolling until stopping an inch before Violet's knees.

"Warrior!" all the guys screamed. Russ stood up and met two of them with gleeful high-fives.

"Go, Vi. Toss it." At Violet's hesitation all the girls chanted for her to make her move. This was her first time in six years that she put her trust in an online dating algorithm. The anxiety was high. But she wanted to connect with her lifemate the same as the rest of them.

"Okay," Violet whispered. She looked up at Russ who was still celebrating and waited for him to lose his big grin. The intensity in his eyes synced with hers and she threw the die.

"Shield." The response among the ladies was far from enthusiastic.

"All right!" Piper boomed. "Next couple."

This wasn't a competition. This was war.

COMMANDER RENT

"Last year in space." He fell back into the raised captain's chair and glanced at Junior Commander Wesson who sat a few spaces lower in the control crater. "Sorry you didn't get called up here sooner, Wes. I know you had spent a good couple years applying for this position."

"I think it's gonna be the wildest battle yet. Can't wait to see how Russell Watke fares. He's a legend in the entire Northern Hemisphere."

"He isn't as brilliant as one might think. Remember that one champion who became a bartender? Russ hangs with him a lot on Earth. Those two are wicked sly and have the intellect of tyrants."

"Meaning what?"

"Neither of them carried their Shields with honor. They like breaking rules."

"So why is Russ still allowed to be here? Because he's your nephew?"

"No." Rent gave an irritated huff. "I want this last woman to change his heart. She has to."

"Nepotism, Commander." Wesson spoke as he fiddled with the color of the lights under the ship's dashboard. "They will see that."

"If he doesn't bring a bride home this time he will be sent to prison. Any crime that has occurred on Sciorlla has been counted as an accident but that is because its laws are lenient. Russell's DNA is everywhere in that soil and he knows it."

"Well, Commander," Wesson said, standing to take a stretch, "let's hope his match is just as crafty as he is."

Rent tapped a dimpled key on the left arm of his chair. "Craftier." The panels framing the panoramic windows lit up neon yellow. "She'll be craftier."

# 3

# Leaving Earth

VIOLET

Changed into the Shield's uniform, Violet followed several of the girls down a corridor at the back of the banquet hall into a massive hangar. Two transports sat ready near the launch tunnel.

"I think they call those Gala Nessas. Bigger than the decades-old Cessna and built for intergalactic travel."

"That's pretty cool." Violet nodded to the girl next to her. It was Megg.

"We talked on the beach, right? "

"Yeah. I'm Violet."

"Oh yeah. The jingle writer. How you liking Russ so far? He's hot, isn't he? "

"Lets see how he does in the game."

"He's a pro at the game, Vi. You better be ready to keep up with him."

"I heard he is wild but I can be wild too."

"You don't seem like the wild type." Megg turned away with a smirk. "I hope you can keep up with the rest of us younger girls."

"Don't worry."  A small-framed girl with mulberry hair stepped in line next to Violet. She fit perfectly in the mandatory uniform, showing braces in her grin. "We aren't all mean girls. Some of us are more mature than others, emotionally speaking. Half these girls just signed up to be with a hot guy. They could care less about a love connection. I'm twenty-six, you're twenty-nine. We're here for serious reasons."

"Agreed. What's your name?"

"Pida. I'm not here to sabotage your chances. I know it looks like one big sorority, but this game is far more than that. I've been to Sciorlla once before."

"What can you tell me about it?"

"As long as you aren't a button masher you can make it to the top five couples."

"Crap." Violet drew in a breath. "I haven't picked up a game controller in three years."

"It'll come back to you," Pida assured. "If you were a gamer once, you'll be one again."


RUSSELL

He circled up with Tuff and Shred behind the transports for one last hurrah on Earth.

"Cheers, mate," Shred said, raising his glass.

Russ grinned and started to follow suit but suddenly cupped his hand over the vodka. His female approached them with a naively curious expression.

"Cricket. Joining in?" he asked her.

His friends traded respecting nods at each other before offering Violet a filled shot glass of her own.  She was unusual for a Shield...dressed in the most understated tomboy fashion yet holding the classic, natural beauty of a female in her last breeding year.

"This is the why the minimum age here is twenty-one. We are all twenty-one, right?" Shred joked. "You sure you aren't eighteen?" He winked at Violet. "Kidding, beauty." He offered a fist bump which she returned. "I'm Shred."

"Violet. Yes, I know I look way younger than twenty-nine."

"At twenty-nine?" Tuff spouted. "Girl, you're smokin' hot!"

They clinked glasses and knocked it back just as Commander Piper called for the boarding to begin.

"Everyone to your assigned transport. Tuff, Violet, you two are on this one. Let's go. Let's go, people."

Russ saw the jitters in his Shield's head and laid a hand on her shoulder. "Hey, babe. Whatever is going on through your head... leave it. Quit thinking so hard. Give yourself permission to act like a hormonal high schooler again."

"I was a bookworm who sat alone at lunch."

"Then be the other girls. Be the wild, fun one." He turned her stiff, trembling body to face him and leaned in close, pressing one hand to her cheek. "We are both almost thirty. This is the last six months we will ever have to be crazy again. Show them they can't mess with Violet Acklin."

She nodded, barely reacting to the kiss he planted on her forehead.

"I'll see you there, Cricket." Russ pointed to the pendant around her neck as he backed toward the other transport. "Don't lose it."

VIOLET

The Gala Nessa's interior was hollow except for two rows of

seats on opposite sides. Commander Piper ordered them to sit in boy-girl-boy-girl configuration with both rows having seven each. Fourteen in the core of each transport. Violet found herself strapped in between Russ's friend Tuff and another guy who seemed to create a tilt in the interior with his wide frame. He wore an extra big smile and heavy-framed glasses.

"First time leaving Earth?"

"Do I look nervous?"

The wide-bodied, thick-spectacled guy laughed in a way that perfectly matched his throaty voice.

"You look like you're about to wet yourself or your booze is about to come up."

"Embarrassing it's that obvious," Violet said. She tried to laugh at herself.

"No worries. I'm Rivet."

"Violet."

They stared at the seven guys and gals across from them, an attitude of superiority taking hold of every single person in the space.

"How much is this thing going to spin?"

"Depends how much the boys bribed the pilot to barrel roll."

"Listen up!" Commander Piper moved briskly down the center of the transport, stopping in front of Violet. "If you know what a proper rollercoaster feels like then you will be able to handle this. Don't hold your breath, don't lean forward. Seven of you are seated against the right wall, seven on the left. You will remain facing each other as your seats do not swivel. If you don't like who you are next to or who is staring at you across the way then you just gotta suck it up. You're stuck with most of these people for six months." He raised his voice in the slightest tone as he went on. "There is always a twenty percent chance of failure to launch and land in this craft. Yes, this thing will spin upside down. That's why everyone has extra protection as far as safety harnesses go. None of you here are trained for intergalactic travel or even survival on another planet. You are video gamers, bookworms, and very uncoordinated athletes. This launch is the first training section. Have fun but please don't be stupid and unbuckle yourself or anyone else during the flight.

Ladies, there is no shame in puking. You will feel nauseous if you have never been in space before. Usually it is the boys who respond the best to the initial trip. Don't fear the sensations. Everyone hears me?"

"Yes, Commander."

"Three minutes to launch. Lock doors, Remy!" he called up to the pilot. He checked each person to see they were secured in their seats before going up to the co-pilot's chair.

Violet sought a look of confidence from her new pal Rivet and he smiled back at her. "Ready?"

"I don't know, Rivet. Can anyone be prepared for this feeling?"

He took off his glasses and stuffed them in the front pocket of his uniform. "Just scream, girl. This is the ride of your life."

Violet closed her eyes and amidst the excited whistles and hollering around her she found her war cry. Leaving Earth for the first and only time in the company of immature, lovestruck, hormonal collegians. It had to be worth it. It had to be what freedom felt like. In the moment she opened her eyes she was upside down.

# 4

# Orientation

COMMANDER RENT

The local time was 3 AM. He watched the recruits file out of the transports onto the ground of Sciorlla. Some of them gazed up at the Zippermare where she hovered in the atmosphere with her lights dimmed in the stars, others kicked the dirt around like school kids fascinated with how similar it felt to Earth. A few of them stood bent over, puking up a stream of green. Rent held up his translucent tablet against the moonlight to do the final count:

***Warriors***

*Larkspur. Age 24.*

*Magnet. Age 21.*

*Airfoil. Age 22.*

*Firewall. Age 25.*

*Granite. Age 26.*

*Hypoxian. Age 25.*

*Gabbro. Age 21.*

*Crosswind. Age 24.*

*Torque. Age 22.*
*Igneous. Age 25.*
*Rivet. Age 24.*
*Shred. Age 26.*
*Tuff. Age 25.*
*Russell. Age 29.*
**Shields**
*Seahorse. Age 23.*
*Corral. Age 21.*
*Holly. Age 25.*
*Megg. Age 22.*
*Agape. Age 22.*
*Alyssum. Age 26.*
*Fahrenheit. Age 24.*
*Eva. Age 21.*
*Harmony. Age 24.*
*Peaches. Age 23.*
*Aura. Age 24.*
*Pida. Age 26.*
*Glory. Age 24.*
*Violet. Age 29.*

"Ladies and gentlemen," he announced into the chilled air. "You will follow me into the mess hall of the Ember D base for further instruction. Each one of you has already been assigned a sleep room and a custom key. The atmosphere here is very much similar to our Earth so do not fear breathing normally."

He turned his back, aware of Wesson watching them from up in the Zippermare cockpit.

RUSSELL

Nothing was new to Russ. Every smell, sight, and vibration on the planet of Sciorlla was home to him.

"Hey, Vi." He touched her shoulder as she stood gaping up at the stars.

"Hey." She barely reacted to his touch.

"It's mesmerizing out here," Russ said. "But it gets even better in the daylight."

"The silence is incredible. The gleam of the constellations against the ink sky is nothing I've seen before."

"Listen, Cricket. I hope you really did your homework before signing up."

Violet finally lowered her eyes and looked directly at him. "What?"

"This isn't a trip of leisure, babe. It's us as a couple against all of them." He pointed toward where everyone was entering the base house. "I need you to channel every bit of nerve you have and propel us to the end."

"Sure. I'll do what I can, Russ," she said.

"Mr. Watke, Miss Acklin, please join us," Rent stated at the doorway. "Use what evening time you can for rest. There are plenty of daylight hours ahead for bonding."

VIOLET

The mess hall inside the base camp was a wide rectangle housing only two long tables and a third section along the wall where Violet assumed was for the hopefully three meals a day.

"Everyone, if you will please take a seat so we can begin the orientation. My spiel shouldn't take more than thirty minutes and you will be shown your rooms."

"Hey, Russ." Rivet poked his arm across the table. "Your Shield handled the transport brilliantly. She is a total space woman."

Violet received a serious stare from Russ before he leaned in and kissed her ear. "Proud of you, Cricket."

Violet shyly looked up at Rivet and his Shield Aura who wouldn't stop nuzzling his face. "I appreciate the compliment."

"All deserved," Rivet said. He turned to Aura and pushed her off him. "Babe, can you please cool it down? I don't even know your favorite dessert yet and you're halfway to unbuttoning my collar."

Aura just giggled and laid her head on his shoulder, wrapping her arms tight around him.

"C'mon, bro," Russ said, laying an arm across Violet's shoulders. "Isn't this part of the package? Cute girls and all the time in the world to get cozy?"

Rivet rolled his eyes and then half-smiled at Violet. "Least yours is waiting for lights out."

Russ gave him a fist bump over the table and then turned to Violet. "What do you think? Too early for spooning in the mess hall?"

"I shouldn't say," Violet said. "My values are probably not shared at this table."

She got several perplexed looks from the guys and gals around her before Commander Rent's voice echoed in the hall.

"Shut up your small talk and listen here."

Violet liked how Rent appeared to be a graceful grandfather type in his faded silver uniform and polished boots, and yet he addressed them all with a youthful, vigorous bark that mismatched his grey hair and pale ocean eyes.

"This is not summer camp. This is not a university dorm. This is not even comparable to spring break. My name, if you did not hear it, is Rent. You would be ordered to call me Commander but since we have Commander Piper with us as well, it is acceptable for you to refer to us as Rent and Piper. Junior Commander Wesson will be introduced to you in due time as he is currently occupied with managing the main ship Zippermare."

Violet noticed the silence in the hall. The respect these people had for Rent surprised her. They were actually listening, each one leaning forward in the most eager and intense way.

"Bullet Rain wakes you up. It is proof of you being worthy of your partner or not. Those of you who are twenty-nine know it is your last time here on Sciorlla. Your final opportunity for a life mate. The rules of the Northern Hemisphere state that twenty-nine years old is the cut off for getting a legal marriage certificate and for conceiving children. Let me reiterate this, people. It is not my law. But you have a chance to assure a bond with your love here and I would not waste a second getting to know that person holding your hand."

Rent looked directly at Violet and she watched his eyes shift from her to Russ. His head tilted in a subtle nod as he continued.

"Not all of you will make it to the end. Only one couple wins the game. Those who chose to bow out back on Earth were perhaps the wisest of you all. They didn't want to risk their lives on another planet to endure a whole new type of survival. The twenty-eight of you here have a chance to make something extraordinary happen in regards to a future for yourself. And for those of you young ones who think you have more time to find your life mate...you must be aware that this is the last year of operation for Ember Dice. Earth's government network is not in favor of us going forward another year, and we must respect the laws of our home planet."

Violet wondered the reasons for the dating site to shut down after so long. She glanced around at the couples sitting and listening to the commander. Everyone seemed light-hearted and cuddly. There wasn't a sense of animosity or danger despite the darkness of Rent's words.

"Let's move onto the fun stuff, shall we?" Rent suddenly had a perky lift in his voice as he shifted from what sounded like a morose disclaimer to a camp counselor giving an energetic rundown of events.

"This is your new schedule hour by hour for the next six months," he said with a mischievous smile, reading from his glowing tablet. "Your wake up call is five o'clock."

"Five in the morning?" One of the Warriors griped from the other long table.

"Five in the morning, yes, Gabbro." Rent held up one hand before the bouncing twenty-one-year-old could say anything more. "Do you need the restroom, son, or are you just fidgeting?"

"I have a sensitive system."

Rent masked a look of disgust by clearing his throat and looking down at the tablet. "Wait for the room assignments. There's a toilet in there." He shook his head before returning to the routine. "Physical training is timed from five to seven and then you will come here for breakfast which spans an hour. Eight to nine. The main portion of each day is the virtual gaming which you will be doing on board the Zippermare from nine am to six pm. Lunch will be brought to you during your game time."

Whispers in the hall started up again as the girls started swapping stories of how good they are at specific video games and guys high-fived each other as they discussed early strategies. Violet felt excitement from everyone and it was contagious. She found herself smiling at Russ as he held her hand under the table.

"Dinner is from six to seven and at that time you will return to the mess hall here. You will have leisure time from seven to nine pm in which you may explore the outside and have any other snacks in the mess hall, as well as being permitted extra virtual game time in the Zippermare. A reminder, people, that no emails or texting is allowed from now until the last day. If a message to Earth is necessary, one of the commanders will send it for you. Nine pm is lights out and at that time you must remain in your sleep room until the wake up call. I will be showing the Shields their rooms and Piper will lead the Warriors to theirs."

COMMANDER RENT

He led the ladies down the corridor and halted in front of one of several doors.

"Every room has a bathroom corner and queen bed. There are no cameras in here. You all lock your own doors with your key pendant which I will assign to you right now."

Rent passed out one key to each Shield and they put them around their necks. "Now," he said, "you are responsible for your own safety and quality of rest each night. I do not expect top performance from you on the first sunrise since it's already near four am, but you will be able to catch up on proper sleep in the coming days." He held up his own key to the door handle and it swung open. "Lights out means we commanders are off duty and unless you wander out into the hall or outside for any reason at those hours, we cannot see you. You are adults and your judgment is yours alone. Violet Acklin."

Violet, the curiously quiet, curly-haired partner to Russ, stepped forward out of the group. "Commander," she said in absolute respect.

"This is your room here, love. 31AJ."

"Where is Russ staying?" she asked.

Rent pointed down the corridor to where the mess hall was. "The Warriors are on the other side. We keep you separate to encourage personal safety and a clear head. Remember, Miss Acklin, this is a competition. Always watch your back." He bent down and spoke low for only her ears. "Be a good Shield but never sacrifice your dignity."

Violet nodded and went into her room, locking the door behind her. Rent moved on with the other Shields, putting each in their rooms and going back out to the Zippermare where Wesson was snoring in the cockpit with an empty family size pizza box halfway off his lap.

"What is with this girl?" he asked himself. "She isn't lasting one week in the game."

# 5

# Day One

RUSSELL

The alarm that blasted into the hall was ear-piercing and Russ could hear several thuds against the walls of his sleep room as the guys literally tumbled out of bed. He knew the routine by heart and without hesitation rolled over to flick on the retina-searing ceiling light. He pulled his uniform on and went out down the corridor to the exit leading outside.

"Let's go, let's go, let's go," Rent shouted. He paced on a raised concrete platform at one corner of a mile of flat green terrain. "Sleep-deprived or not I wanna see some skill today. Warriors, Shields, line up for the first sprint."

Russ kept an eye out for his friends as they slowly emerged from inside Ember D. Most had a sleepy face and awkward gait as they approached the field.

"It'd be cooler if we did this in a stadium," one of the guys said.

"You mean with screaming fans?"

"I wish my mom could see me now," Gabbro said proudly as

he straightened his shoulders in the line formation.

"Your only audience," Russ spoke to them, "are the commanders. Heads down, Warriors."

Violet appeared to his left, looking bright-eyed and full of nervous energy as she stared at the horizon. Russ stepped in line beside her and turned his eyes forward. "Do you know anything about space?"

"I'm probably the least astronomical one here," she admitted.

"Then you have a long six months ahead, don't you?"

"I'm not afraid, Russ. We're in this together."

Russ blew out a long breath and watched the cold air form a cloud in front of him. "My Shield." He faced her. "The atmosphere may feel like Earth but the rules here are nothing like home." He bumped his shoulder hard into her chest as he went to rejoin his friends.


VIOLET

Rumors had spread through the girls that she was a matte snake. Violet imagined that any one of her fellow Shields could have learned the story and taken it through the hive of queen bees acting all superior on the field with their glittery eye makeup and show-stopping magenta lipstick. It was a morning of physical training and Violet was the only girl who stepped outside in the basic uniform sans makeup, battered sneakers and tangled hair. The rest of them looked ready for a charity ball.

"Is it true, girl?" Megg pressed her. "Are you really with the underground mattes?"

"Let's just run," Violet said.

"She's a matte snake," Aura called out to the boys. "Violet Acklin is a total weapons hoarder."

Violet glowered at both of them as she got in line next to Russ.

"Attention here, people." Rent stood with a bullhorn on his platform flanked by Commander Piper and a slightly younger fellow with moose brown hair that made his head looked like he had just been struck by lightning. "Junior Commander Wesson has come down from the ship to observe the first test of the recruits. Wesson, Piper, and I are here for all of you and this is just the start. This is a sprint, not a marathon. Speed is what matters today."


COMMANDER RENT

"Who are you betting on, sir?" Wesson asked Piper.

"Who do I think will be in the lead or who do I think will bring up the rear?"

"No, sir. Who are you betting on to be the dark horse?"

"My dollars are on either Rivet or Violet. That Warrior is the least likely to excel in any physical activity but he is no doubt a champion gamer. And Miss Acklin...she is one to watch."

"Why her? She is the most plain-dressed, unassuming female out there."

"Piper loves the underdog, Wes," Rent said. "But I have to agree with you. Violet doesn't seem to be prepared for this sort of competition."

"A woman doesn't have to appear perfect to be a capable fighter. I say she leads the pack on the first sprint."

"I bet she doesn't." Wesson traded smirks with Rent as they crossed to the very edge of the platform.

"Run at the sound of the siren!" Rent called out. "Three, two, one."


VIOLET

The butterflies in her stomach rose at the siren and her vision tunneled. Everyone left and right of Violet stalled as she bolted to the front, creating a picturesque V-formation on the field. The bodies around her disappeared into a haze as she showed them who she was and why she belonged in the game.

RUSSELL

"Again! Run again!" Rent was shouting. He waved his arms for them to return to the starting line.

"Is he pulling our leg?" Rivet gasped, breathless, hunched over as he followed Russ back across the field. "One sprint is enough, isn't it?"

Russ looked over at where Violet had ended her run. She was very slowly turning around to go back to the start, all the other Shields eyeing her with annoyance and shock.

"She just smoked us," Tuff said, gleefully. "Russ, aren't you glad you picked that one?"

"It's just one sprint," Russ said back. "She can't do it again."

Everyone lined up again for a second sprint and the siren went off. Violet shot out in front as she had done the first time and Russ pushed himself to keep up. Tuff ran alongside him, shouting between hard breaths. "Tomboy and moral princess all in one powerhouse."

COMMANDER RENT

Wesson tilted his head to one side as the Shields and Warriors walked back from the second sprint. "Violet Acklin," he said aloud. "Such a plain, unassuming lady."

"After she ran like that?" Piper asked. "Miss Acklin is a tigress."

"I've never seen speed like that by anyone. An early morning run with that sort of confidence?" Rent stepped down off the platform. "She needs to be tested."

He called out to Russ and Violet and motioned for them to follow him. "The rest of you go to the mess hall."

Russ was ordered to stand at the doorway of the testing room as Rent, Piper, and Wesson had gathered in the lowest section of the Zippermare which housed sections for emergency evacuation equipment, medical testing, and a freezer full of expired pizzas. Violet's expression of confusion remained as Rent spoke to her in a stern voice.

"Miss Acklin, your performance out there was astounding. Beyond astounding. It was impossible."

"Improbable," Wesson corrected.

"No." Rent gave him a sharp glance. "Impossible. No one runs with that much speed right after they arrive. And your eyes," he said to Violet, "are so awake and vibrant. None of you got proper rest. It is only fair to know what you have in your system."

"Do what you have to," Violet said. "I'm not on drugs. I just love to run."

Piper assisted in utilizing the needle to attain her blood and Violet calmly sat through the process, body relaxed under the bright lights of Zippermare's deepest floor. She looked at Russ who continued to stand in the doorway across the room, his eyes staring dead serious back at her.

Within fifteen minutes of staggering silence, Rent and Piper traded smirks after tapping on the computer screen across from Violet's chair. "Well now," Rent said. "You really are just a little spitfire, girl."

"Clean?" Wesson asked.

"Pure blood. Pure everything. She's good to go," Piper said.

He gave Violet a hand to help her slide off the raised-up testing chair.

"Wait a moment, Miss Acklin." Rent stepped between her and Russ. "Is it true that you are a matte snake?"

Violet appeared panicked. "Where did you hear that?"

"Are you a matte snake? I need an honest answer now."

"The other girls were talking about me but I promise I'm not a threat to anyone."

"Are you carrying a weapon?" Rent asked.

"She really is from the underground crew?" Wesson's eyes were wide. He grinned. "The government network hates your type, Shield. You'll be jailed back home."

Violet held up her hands and took a step backward. "Yes. I am carrying."

"Give it over." Rent spread his palms in front of her and waited. She reached behind her and pulled a pistol from the seat of her uniform pants.

"Matte snake," Wesson whispered and giggled.

"Here." Violet furrowed her eyebrows and handed it to Rent. "I'm not here to make trouble, sir. I just bring what makes me comfortable."

"I won't report this discovery to anyone outside, Miss Acklin. Sciorlla law protects your secrets. But you may not have any other weapons found on you or you will be sent home."

"Understood, Commander Rent." She stood straight before giving a deep bow that caused all three Ember Dice officials to chuckle.

"What was that for, love?" Rent asked as Violet headed out of the room with Russ.

"Respect," she said over her shoulder. "Goes both ways."

Rent watched on the video screen as the Warrior and Shield

went into the mess hall.

"So," he said, turning to Wesson. "Still think she's unassuming?"


VIOLET

Most of the Shields and Warriors were halfway through eating their breakfast when she got in line ahead of Russ to pick over the buffet.

"Why you got a gun, Cricket?" he whispered. "You're safe with me."

"Safety isn't why I carry," Violet said. "It's my identity back home. But nobody else here will agree with me."

"Keep your head down and play the game." Russ swatted her on the butt as he slid his cream-filled coffee onto his tray and went to join the Warriors.

Violet picked up a blueberry muffin, granola bar, and hash browns before stopping at the coffee. She didn't notice Rivet walking up to refill his cup.

"Wow. You drinking it black?"

"Yup." Violet held the tray with one hand and lifted her coffee to her mouth with the other. She smiled as she tasted it.

"Hardcore, girl. That stuff tastes like jet fuel."

"Morning jolt," she said, raising her cup in a toast as she started toward the table filled with twittering, fluttering Shields. She realized they were all purposefully circled up at one end, a secret conversation in progress. All of them except for Pida who gave Violet a smile and scooted down with her tray.

"Can you tell me how you did that?"

"Do what?"

"How did you run so fast? I suck at all the athletic stuff and have been terrible at it since junior high."

Violet sipped her black coffee before answering Pida. "It's gonna sounds bookworm geeky but I pretend orcs are chasing me."

"Orcs?"

"I'm more a literary nerd than a game nerd. Not proud of my gun secret coming out either." Violet stabbed a clump of hash brown. "I didn't plan on becoming the gamer pariah right out the gate here."

"Don't worry about it. I think it's cool. At least we have a real soldier on our side this time. Women aren't encouraged to pick up weapons on Earth anymore."

"Yeah." Violet pushed the muffin crumbs to the edge of her plate. "Sucks we aren't allowed arms on Sciorlla."

"You don't trust your Warrior?"

Violet kept her voice low. "I don't trust the other girls."


RUSSELL

"I knew she had a gun," Shred said. "She always looks like she has her guard up."

"Maybe because she knows Russ is a jinx."

"Not a jinx," Russ said.

"So you say." Rivet leaned over to steal a waffle square from Tuff's plate. "Last girl you matched with was twenty-two and she died during the first round of the Dash Riff while you were flying it. Do we still call it an accident?"

"I'm not a death trap." Russ gave the guys an intense stare over his coffee cup. "Just unlucky."

"You're lucky to have Vi as your partner. She's a beast on the field. I can't wait to see how she does in the virtual world."

Russ snarled as he forked up a bite of sausage.

"Whats wrong with you?" Tuff asked.

"He's jealous," Gabbro said. "Because we all got owned by a Shield in the first hour."

Igneous, the classic dork with warped glasses and theatrical overbite, spoke his wisdom from the other side of the table. "A Shield's job is to stay in front of her Warrior.  Far as I'm concerned, Violet did exactly what she is supposed to do by running ahead of you."

"She didn't have to outshine all of us, bro." Rivet looked at his agitated friend. "That's why you're jealous."

"No, Rivet," Russ said, wiping his mouth with a napkin. "I'm not jealous of my Shield.  But I hope she is just as good at everything else. We have six months, boys. Six months to prove we can stay or go home." He stood, picking up his coffee and looking straight down into the cup. "Time for more jet fuel."

# 6

# Virtual World

RUSSELL

Nine o'clock signaled the start of the gaming. The Warriors led their Shields onto the Zippermare and Junior Commander Wesson steadied her to hover high in the air above Sciorlla. Several paces west from the front cockpit was the gaming sector at the backside of the Zippermare. Each couple was told to sit in their own tiny rooms with walls dividing each pair. Massive video screens were in front of them as they sat in the highest-grade game chairs which included headsets, every type of controller and button invented, and situated so closely that if one wanted they could sit on each other's lap during gameplay.

Commander Piper stood right behind the cockpit, speaking to everyone through his own headset as he stared into the dark void of space outside the panoramic window. He flicked a switch to his right and each screen lit up in the gaming pods. Split screen game-play was the standard and made focusing on your individual avatar a priority.

Russ saw Violet wide-eyed and giddy next to him and he squeezed her hand tight as Piper began the introduction.

"Ready?"

"I am," she said.

"Eyes forward, babe. Let's crush this."

VIOLET

The game room glowed blue from the lights on the floor and the frame of the video screen.

"You will design your avatar first," Piper was saying. "I will explain the rules and etiquette while you do so."

Violet concentrated on the hairstyle and clothing of her female avatar as she heard the other Shields swapping ideas through her headphones. Everyone on board the Zippermare could hear the chatter of each Shield and Warrior and the displays in each gaming pod, all fourteen of them, were cast onto the main screen of the ship for Commander Piper and Junior Wesson to keep track of the progress.

"There are ten levels in Bullet Mate. Each of you must master the buttons, joysticks, and analog sticks in order to successfully complete the game. Each level contains one main battle that you have to win three times in order to move onto the next level. You can have as many attempts as you need but you must finish as a team three times alive. We call this the Trio Finish."

Russell had already finished his avatar and sat on the edge of his seat waiting for Piper to finish the introduction.

"You are playing against real people from all over the galaxy. There is no pause button. If you die, your avatar will regenerate within five seconds on screen in the same position. Shields, your aim is to stay ahead of your partner. You protect him. Stay alert to whatever pops out in the corners of the screen. Warriors, if you aim poorly you will kill your Shield. Keep a steady hand. Your Shields protect you so you protect them. If any pair completes all ten levels successfully ahead of everyone else, it doesn't mean you get extra lazy time. At that point you will log extra training hours for the real world battle. Let's take a look at the levels, recruits."

The on-screen display listed the Bullet Rain levels as follows:

1. *The Old Guard: An open world ground battle. Combat Style: Old world weapons*
2. *Ocean Rogue: An underwater and aquatic surface fight. Combat Style: Old world and modern tech weapons.*
3. *RaceTrak 1.0: A classic car chase battle sequence. Combat Style: Automatic weapons.*
4. *Clock Fire: Kill the enemy before time is up and the volcano erupts. Combat Style: Old world weapons and modern tech weapons.*
5. *Freefall Felon: A fight in the clouds, on top of a jet. Combat Style: Modern tech weapons.*
6. *Sniper Tree: A basic hunt for the enemy. Combat Style: Rifles*
7. *Zero-G Rumble: Avatars floating in space must be controlled within spins and flips as they are fired upon by the enemy. Combat Style: Space pistols.*
8. *RaceTrak 2.0: Car chase involving a hijacking of three different vehicles before evading. Combat Style: Modern tech weapons.*
9. *Sky War: A fight inside a jumbo jet or helicopter. Combat Style: Modern tech weapons.*
10. *Bullet Rain: The title game which involves every pair lining up on their screens and charging against the enemy line for the ultimate battle. Combat Style: Every weapon allowed.*

"Some of you here have played this game many times and some

of you are absolute novices. The only advice I have from here on out, ladies and gentlemen, is to fight dirty on the screen and follow the rules in the real world. There is more than one way to be disqualified here on Sciorlla. Do not throw your partner under the bus for any reason or you both will be sent home."

Violet looked quickly at Russ who calmly turned his head.

"What's wrong?" he asked.

"How do we get disqualified?"

"You won't, Cricket. You'll be fine."

"But how does it happen?"

Russ rolled his eyes and took the headset off his head to answer her in a whisper. "If the commanders find out partners are sabotaging each other, it will mean an immediate elimination for both of them. If either one of us were to dislike the other and feel like it's not a good match-up, telling the truth of that to Piper or Rent would mean we forfeit the game." He leaned in and kissed her cheek. "But I never lose."


COMMANDER RENT

Rent sat in the mess hall, scrolling through background information on his tablet. He wore his own headset to add input and listen to the activity on the Zippermare.

"Piper, how's Miss Acklin doing in the practice level?"

"Struggling," Piper said. "She's got weak hand eye coordination."

"Russ. Is he doing his thing?"

"As always he is accelerating through it. The boy is gifted."

"Not looking promising for this Shield chained to his hip."

"Don't be sure of anything," Piper said. "We have several hours left of this first day and you know the history of the Shields."

Rent stood up, placing his tablet on the long table. He looked toward the exit of the mess hall. "All right, Piper. She may still be the one."

# 7

# The Dash Riff



At the conclusion of an uneventful dinner, Commander Rent made the announcement that everyone was to follow him to the hangar set on the far end of the running field. It was time to introduce the Dash Riff.

"Each couple must strap themselves into their craft before further instruction. You will both get a turn at piloting the controls once in space. Russ and Violet will be the first pair to go out, and on my signal the rest of you will follow."

Violet slid into the cockpit and Russ sealed the doors. "So this is the Dash Riff?" she asked.

"It is. The bottom of the craft is stronger than the top so we have to train to fly inverted over the enemy."

"Who's the enemy?"

Russ reached across her to flick the exterior light switch on. It was a tight fit in the Riff, no room for armrests or to stretch one's legs. Violet's questions irritated him the same as the past Shields had.

"The commanders have us practice sky drills in case of an

attack from outside the planet. We team up against Sciorlla natives and fire ammunition while utilizing the proper dives and speed tactics."

"Real ammo?"

"No. Shots fired are harmless to both sides. It's just a drill." Russ dug under his seat to find a pack of hot pepper gum. "Before you ask me another question, Cricket, keep in mind that every lesson you learn here is necessary for the final battle on Sciorlla. And Sciorlla natives are watching all of us from up there." He pointed out at the night sky.

Violet looked confused. "Why would the original inhabitants of this planet matter to Ember Dice?"

"Because," Russ said, pressing in the ignition button, "I know one of them personally. A Sciorllan trusts me to protect this planet after the company shuts the program down. Our alliance with them matters more now than ever."

"Who's this Sciorllan friend, Russ?"

"His name is Ark."

VIOLET

She wondered what Russ was alluding to in his concerns for Sciorlla but at the same moment all she wanted was to experience the thrill of the Dash Riff.

"Check straps and helmet," Russ said. "Try to vomit in the bag and not on me."

"You assume I'm gonna puke before we are off the ground?"

Russ smirked as he revved the accelerator gear. "Every Shield who rode with me had a weak stomach. It's either them or I'm just a mad hornet in the air."

"I loved the ride on the Gala Nessa. Not afraid of blacking out or throwing up."

"Good. Hang on, babe."

A low-pitched hum filled the cockpit as Russ piloted the space craft up into a steep angle. Within seconds he flipped them upside down and Violet released a gleeful shriek and giggles.

"Ascension complete," Russ said into the headset.

"Stand by for the sky drill," Rent responded.

There was a long wait for the other couples to fly up in their crafts and Violet noticed how isolated and dark it was sitting in the void of outer space.

"Do you ever get used to the darkness up here?"

"Afraid?" Russ asked with a chuckle.

"No, just amazed. The night sky never looks this lifeless from Earth."

"Sure doesn't, Cricket. This is deep space."

Violet grinned. "I like it. Although," she said, looking down, "it's a tight squeeze in here."

"Built for making out," Russ said. He whipped his head to face her and leaned in to touch his mouth to hers. Violet blushed while she kissed him back.

"And this," Russ said as he glanced at the lower control panel, "is why I love Ember Dice." He stroked the side of her face as she looked into his eyes. "We couldn't do this on an Earth date."

They leaned into each other for more gentle kisses until the voice of Rent sounded over their headsets.

"Sky drill one, Russell Watke. Show the others how it's done."

Russ noticed the group of Dash Riffs sitting in formation behind them. Without a word, he offered Violet a piece of hot pepper gum. She took it and blushed even harder.

RUSSELL

"There they are, babe. The incoming ships."

His Shield looked completely unfocused as she unwrapped the piece of gum. Her fingers were shaking.

"Cricket, you good? I need you to fire the ammo."

"Yeah, sorry." She looked up quickly and looked back down. "I haven't been kissed like that in a long time."

Russ smirked. "You were a late bloomer, weren't you?"

"Never mind that," Violet said. "But I have a proposition, Russ. Let me be the pilot."

"You're trembling so much there's no way you could steer this."

"Let me do it."

The firm tone in her voice sounded out of character and Russ chewed his spicy gum hard as he gave it a thought. He threw his hands up. "All right, babe. Have at it."

They had to crawl over each other to switch seats and Violet suddenly appeared like an expert at the wheel.

"Upside down!" Russ started to yell as they approached the Sciorllan fleet. Violet touched each control with perfect precision as she not only flew but fired upon the enemy.

"How did you know all this?" Russ asked. "You've never been in one of these before!"

"I never told you," Violet said in a braggart's voice. "I raced cars back home."

"This isn't a car, you dork."

"Sure feels similar to me!"

# 8

# Commanders

COMMANDER RENT

Wesson poured coffee into three mugs in the ship's kitchenette. A new day of virtual gaming was underway on the Zippermare.

"Did you hear that Violet kicked their butts in archery this morning?"

"I was there, Wes," Rent said. "I saw."

"She looked really sexy doing it," Wesson said. He sipped his coffee and grinned at Rent and Piper who were both getting their morning exercise in on rebound trampolines. "You guys look like dorks."

"Wes," Piper said between bounces, "I thought you didn't like tomboys."

"Vi is a natural athlete. I can't help what I like."

"Tomboy."

"No. She's a Fighter Princess."

"Can't be crushing on a Warrior's woman, son," Piper said.

"I'm not. But Russ doesn't seem that in love with her."

"Too early for love," Rent said. "Give it time."

"If Miss Acklin dies, it'll be the fourteenth Shield on his hands. It's gonna happen again, Rent."

"What are you talking about?" Wesson asked Piper. He looked at Rent who finally stepped off his little trampoline. "What's this death curse Russell Watke has on Shields?"

"Russ had anger management problems from the first day I took him in my care. It's been a possible factor in his unfortunate game incidents. If you didn't know, Wes, I'm his uncle. Not blood uncle."

"Yeah, you told me. So what's this problem? He's easily ticked off or what? Did you ever send him to a psych center?"

"No, no." Rent shook his head. "No, Wes. It has never been confirmed that he is a danger of any kind."

Piper took a mug from the counter and paced in front of the cockpit.

"You won't protect Russ again, will you?"

"He trusts me to have his back."

"He's a grown-ass man, Rent."

"He never wanted to take his meds and I'm not going to force it after this whole program ends either."

"If Violet's life ends on this planet, we will all be put on trial."

# 9

## Night

VIOLET

The knock came out of nowhere and half-asleep Violet opened her bedroom door to get rammed into by Russ. The adrenaline woke her up faster than his rough hands pressing against her mouth.

"Listen to me," he said. His eyes were wild as he tried to pin her on the bed. "Don't say anything. You leave this room and we both get sent home."

Violet gripped his wrists and pulled him up and away from her body. She felt his muscles strain against her. "Russ, what are you doing?"

"C'mon, Vi. I need alone time with you. C'mon. Let's have some fun."

"No. No, you get away from me."

The grin that appeared on his face looked unnatural. "Kiss me, Cricket."

"Get out of my room." Violet pushed her entire body weight against Russ as he still tried to lay on top of her. She kept her voice low as she struggled. "I smell alcohol. You're totally drunk.”

"I'm in love with you. I want you," Russ purred.

"Get off me, Russell."  She smacked him flat against the forehead and once more on the edge of his nose.  He flailed, catching himself.

"Babe, c'mon. What the heck?" He crawled forward, giggling in a high-pitched voice. "You're freakin hot."

Violet threw a punch straight into the bridge of his nose, scrambling onto her bed and standing up, holding an unplugged lamp over her head. Russ dropped against the door.

"Ow. Damn Shields."


RUSSELL

He went out into the corridor, purposely glancing toward the camera.  The commanders saw everything outside the rooms. Surely Rent was awake and watching the insanity from the Zippermare.

"Rivet, bro, wake up."

He wasn't certain he was knocking on Rivet's door but the occupant of the room let him in. It was indeed Rivet standing there, fumbling to put his glasses on.

"What happened? Do I have to run an extra lap?"

Russ bounced in place. "I just did a thing with Violet."

"Yeah okay, but we're sleeping."

"No, I went to her room and she let me in. We had a cuddle."

Rivet stared, wiped dried drool from the side of his face, and tilted his head, glasses sliding.  "She let you in for a cuddle?" He sounded like he was still dreaming on his pillow. "Man, it's two-thirty." He lifted an arm and tapped his wrist.

"We did." Russ giggled as he stepped in further, eyes widening as he held a hand to his throbbing, bloody nose.

"No. You did not." Rivet shook the sleep from his head and started to realize what was going on. "You attacked her. You attacked your Shield, didn't you?"

"No, Rivet. I swear I did not." He was completely serious and within five seconds burst out laughing and fell on Rivet's bed.

"Okay, tell me after morning training." Rivet grumbled to himself as he laid down on the floor. "Sleep it off, maniac."

"Someone put drugs in the vodka!" Russ shouted amidst his uncontrollable laughter. "I've been sabotaged."

VIOLET

No one said a word to each other during the morning sprint and archery drills. Violet kept her head down, refusing to look at Russ as he smiled into the Sciorllan sun like he was an untouchable king of the planet. The silence ended at breakfast.

Violet had planted herself between Pida and Glory at their table, hoping to quell any rumors about herself before they dropped. Commander Rent's announcement came out sharply, causing a few of them to jump. He never entered the mess hall in the morning and his tone of voice was unusual.

"It has come to my attention that an illegal substance has been hidden within two sleep pods. Crosswind, you and your Shield Eva must come with me."

People went from stuffing faces to gaping at the sheepish couple forced to follow Rent out of the mess hall. Once they were out of sight, the commotion started up again.

"Did you think he had drugs? He doesn't even drink regular beer. Why would he smoke?"

"What if it was needles? You think they found vials in his room?"

"Eva can't be kicked out! She didn't do anything!"

Violet saw Russ staring intently at her from the other table, his arm casually draped over the back of his chair. He lifted a finger to his lips as she started to open her mouth.

"Hey," Pida said. "How come Russ is all beat up? His face looks like a banged-up plum."

Violet covered her mouth as she choked back a giggle.

"So they both go home even if it was only Crosswind who brought drugs?" Glory asked. "How is that fair?"

"Sciorlla rules," Aura said as she chewed toast.

"Ember Dice rules," Rivet said loudly as he walked past their table with his tray. "It's over for both of them."

# 10

# Womanizer

VIOLET

"Lookin' good, Aura," Russ called into his headset. Violet saw him wink at the screen and smacked him on the shoulder with her controller.

"Ow, babe. What's wrong with you? Save that for the game."

Violet scooted forward in her seat and faced him. "This IS the game, you womanizer. Stop flirting with the other Shields."

"A compliment is fair. I'll only ever kiss you, Cricket."

"Why do you get to cheer on the other girls?"

"You're being too sensitive."

"Get out of here," Violet said. "Let me play the game alone in this pod."

"I walk out now and we both get sent home. Don't be stupid, darling."

"Don't be stupid, idiot," she snapped back and returned to the screen.

Russ dropped the controller in his lap and spread his hands. "You know I like you, right?"

"Either you steer this car or we switch back to my driving and you shoot out the window. Pick!"

"You are so uptight, girl."

"Shut up."

RUSSELL

Lunchtime in the pods was less about savoring delicious food in space and more about scarfing down cold pizza in order to keep pace in the levels. Every couple seemed to be at a different place in the game and every single person was incredibly vocal despite mouths full of food. The dialogue sounded disgusting.

"Babe, you don't get to pause the level. Just put it in your mouth and pick up the controller. We gotta finish strong. We have one more win to go and we're onto Clock Fire which, frankly, is my favorite level."

"Fine."

Violet still seemed mad that he had chatted up Aura an hour ago and her concentration in the virtual world was suffering because of it.

"Not that one, babe. Use the wheel. You drive, I'll shoot."

"The gun is my job, Russ."

"Your avatar is totally flailing with it out the window. Just point and shoot at the scum coming up behind us."

All at once Violet snarled, jabbed Russ in the chest hard with her elbow, and leaned forward so that her nose touched the screen. Half a slice of lukewarm cheese pizza was folded inside her mouth as she called out.

"Bite me, Warrior."

VIOLET

Dinner in the mess hall proved to be another evening of gossip and flirting between Shields and Warriors.

"Russ baits the ones that have been out of the dating game a long time."

"Yeah, or the ones who never tried online dating. His prey." Aura smiled wide and shrugged her shoulders with a wave of her fork. "Like you, Violet."

"I have done online dating before."

"But it's been a long time, hasn't it? Too many creepers and not enough compatibility to suit the long-term vibe."

"Yup," Violet said, spooning lukewarm veggie soup into her mouth. "Stalkers."

"Since when do you care about quality relationships?" Pida asked Aura. "All you do is blow kisses to the other Warriors. You hardly cozy up to Rivet."

"Eh. He's okay. I mean, yes, he is quality. But do I want to be married to someone like that for the rest of my life?"

"This is our last chance to be up here."

"So what? I can find more on Earth too. Preferably a man like Russ."

The other Shields at the table looked at Violet as Aura smirked. "I think Russell likes me more than he likes you, sweetie."

"I don't like you at all." Violet stood, leaving her tray on the table. She picked up her half-empty glass of orange juice and aggressively took a sip. "And please, Aura, do not call me 'sweetie' again or I'll kick your ass."

In her agitated march toward the front door, Violet felt all eyes follow her and heard a rising current of giggles. The shyness had faded, replaced by a stance of war.

# 11

# Weakness

RUSSELL

"Your arms are shaking, bro."

"I know that, Tuff."

"Just relax. Why do you always freeze up at rifles?"

The Warriors were lined up several paces from soft targets and in this outdoor exercise they had to fire a rifle in front of their Shields before the Shields got a turn. The difference in real world shooting from virtual shooting didn't seem to be a problem for everyone else. Just Russ.

"Down on the ground!" Rent called.

The Shields had to lay on their stomachs for the next shot.

"Russ, chill. Breathe."

Russ growled at the encouragement of his friends. His weakness was still that. His weakness.

"Nice shot, Igneous," Rent said as he paced down the line. "Steady your hand, Russell, or you will never make the target."

"Permission to use the bathroom, Commander."

"Go ahead, son, but you'll miss your Shield in her round of shots."

Russ stood up and gave his rifle to Rent. He walked toward the base to retreat into the facilities, face reddening in humiliation as the Shields all watched him approach.

"Hi, Russ," Aura said with a giggle, blowing him a kiss. Pida punched her in the arm as Violet noticed the flirty interaction.

"She's a jerk, Vi. Don't worry about her," Pida told Violet as they took their places behind the Warriors at the range.

Russ paused in his walk toward the base and considered what he would be missing. The Shields all seemed lively and wound up, making the idea of their target practice an absolutely showstopping affair. The toilet break could wait.

VIOLET

She proved her worth without much thought of the magnificent action behind it. Commander Rent had a prideful, glowing stare as he watched her complete task after task, target after target. Russ, on the other hand, refused to smile. He stayed to watch, but within ten minutes, Violet saw him turn and run toward the mess hall.

RUSSELL

"What do you think about swapping partners?" Russ asked as he grabbed a tray. "Think we could try it?"

Shred frowned as he followed in line. "What's wrong with Vi?"

"He's jealous because she is better than him at the guns," Igneous said, amidst pouring himself a cup of orange juice. "And she is the least superficial of us all. Quite attractive and spirited. You are undeserving, Russell. You are, in the perfect word, faultfinding."

"Shut up, Igneous. Go spew your poetic philosophies to your Shield."

"Well, I would, Russ, but every time I try to speak that way to Peaches, she says I'm all fluff and no substance." Igneous set his tray down and gave a look at the other plates at their table. "I'm gonna get some hash browns."

"See?" Russ sat next to Shred. "That's what I mean. If the females don't like us as we are, they can trade."

"Sure, if it was allowed."

"Who says it isn't, Tuff? I've been swapping Shields for years." Russ half-smiled as they gaped at him.

"Are you for real?"

"Guys, listen to me." He motioned for them to lean in close across the table. "If a Shield flirts with you, take it as a sign. Go with peace and good conscience. Aura likes me. Shred, haven't you heard Glory flirt with you during the virtual gaming?"

VIOLET

Everything at the Shields table was peaceful, a girl once in awhile glancing over to where the Warriors were choking with laughter over some immature dude banter. The usually silent Igneous suddenly yelled from the buffet line.

"Who took all the hash browns? It's my only highlight between now and lunch. I need my hash browns! Can someone spare one?"

Violet and Pida watched in amusement as burly Rivet rush over to sit down between them with his tray. A mountain of hash browns filled his entire plate. He motioned for them not to say anything, but Igneous marched right behind him.

"All right, Rivet. I know you're messing with me. You don't

even like hash browns."

"Sorry, man. I'm starving."

"Could you spare one of your million?"

"Here." Rivet stabbed one with his fork and held it up to Igneous.

"Tomorrow I'm gonna be first in line." Igneous snarled in a pathetic fashion and went back to the other table.

Rivet rolled his eyes and traded smirks with the Shields who all looked at him. "What?"

"That's pretty harsh, my love," Aura said to her Warrior. "I think you should apologize to Igneous."

"I think you should apologize to the other girls here for flirting with their boyfriends, Aura." Rivet raised his eyebrows at her and she scoffed before moving toward the Warrior table.

"Yup. There she goes again."

"Thanks a lot, Rivet," Megg said. "You just sent her back into their arms."

"My bad," Rivet said in a sarcastic voice as he attacked his tower of hash browns with his fork.

"Well, anyway," Violet said, trying to return to her previous conversation with Pida, "I don't know why everyone keeps picking on me for being a matte snake. Why is owning a gun so bad? I just crushed it out there on the field."

"Actually, I think it's hot. I always wanted to date a matte snake."

Aura strutted back over in her custom uniform heels, just in time to see Rivet gazing with admiration at Violet. "Why are you still here?"

"The guys are talking about inappropriate stuff. I don't wanna be a part of that," Rivet said.

"Oh, like how they wanna have fun with the girls in their

room?”

"No. Like swapping partners."

"And I know it's not my business to say, but Russ started it. He's been adding vodka to the coffee."

They all turned in their seats to watch the show going on at the other table. Russ and Tuff were standing on top of it, leading the Warriors in some sort of musical number.

"Yeah, that's real Warrior skill right there." Rivet rolled his eyes.

Violet stifled a giggle.

"I didn't even know Igneous could dance like that," Shield Peaches said, looking completely offended that she had been left out of the performance. "He told me he was as wobbly as a baby giraffe on ice."

Pida burst out laughing, iced tea squirting out of her nose. The uproarious giggling of the Shields caused the Warriors to stop and realize what they had brought upon themselves.

"A toast to stupidity!" Igneous exclaimed, almost toppling over as he joined Tuff and Russ on top of the table. He raised a glass of vodka.

Russ clinked glasses with him and gave a wink to the girls. "Cheers, ladies."

# 12

# Gerald Ark

COMMANDER RENT

Wesson sat in the cockpit with a half-frozen sugar doughnut in hand, his legs propped up on the top panel of buttons. He watched with Rent and Piper as the recruits finished up their mile run and headed in toward the mess hall for breakfast.

"Who is Ark?"

"What?" Rent said.

"Ark. I've heard the name mentioned through my headset. Russ said something about it to Violet when they first went up in the Dash Riff." He shrugged and moved his legs off the controls. "I heard him say Ark."

Rent gave him a stern look, not understanding how the rookie commander could have picked up the name of Gerald Ark. He decided to give an explanation, despite his annoyance at the questions.

"Gerald Ark is a native of Sciorlla who we let into Ember Dice years ago as an experiment across planets."

"And? He didn't turn out well?"

Piper joined in, speaking before Rent finished swallowing his coffee. "He turned out to be an assassin of sorts, never making friends with any of the commanders. But he was permitted to stay on Earth under the guise of a bartender."

"Wait. Not the bartender who Russ talks with," Wesson said.

"That's him."

"I don't fully understand their connection, but I know it's dangerous for the rest of us."

"Sir," said Wesson, "what in the whacked out stars system is that traitor even doing here? Russ should be in prison with Ark if they both committed crimes like that. You actually know that he set up kills down on Earth and you let him keep coming back?"

Rent didn't respond, taking precise steps toward the kitchenette. His shoulders raised and dropped back down in a silent sigh. "I promised Ellk this was his last time. That's why the company is shutting down."

"Because of Russell Watke?" Wesson asked, voice echoing in the ship.

"No. It's Gerald Ark. The Sciorllan extraterrestrial," Piper answered. He moved toward Rent, shaking his head with a somber expression. "He is not who we think he is. He holds the trigger to the biggest detonator on Earth."

"What are you talking about?"

Piper started to respond to Wesson again but Rent gave them both an intense look over his coffee mug as he took a sip. "I'm not going back," he said softly. "None of us are."

VIOLET

Her appetite that morning led to the biggest pile of pancakes, fried eggs, and orange juice she had ever consumed in her twenty-nine years. Pida kept her company on one end of the table, both girls focusing on scarfing down food rather than gossiping about the Shields sitting at the other end.

"Go away, dude."

Violet saw Pida shooing her hands at Rivet as he approached with his tray. "Your Shield will get jealous if you keep talking to us."

"Forget that, Pida," Rivet said. "My Shield flirts with all the Warriors over there. Listen, Vi, we need to talk."

"She's busy." Pida stood up to block him from getting near her.

"No, it's okay." Violet motioned for Rivet to sit across from them. She stuffed a syrupy bite of pancake in her mouth and lifted her half-drunk glass of orange juice as a signal for him to speak.

"Vi, I hate to say this but if Russ tries to hurt you again, please just take the fall and go home."

"Hurt her?" Pida looked wide-eyed at him then at Violet. "When did he do that?"

"Don't worry, Rivet. Nothing happened. He just got a little extra frisky at night."

"Girl, don't pretend that he didn't attack you." Rivet leaned in, his glasses slipping down. "You knocked him good in the nose."

Pida whipped her head to face Violet and gripped her arm in excitement. "You did that?!"

"Shh." Violet held the fork vertical to her lips. "I don't want to get Russ in trouble."

"It's gonna get worse. Believe me," Rivet said.

"You haven't been here that many times. How do you know how bad he gets?" Pida asked him.

Rivet burped and excused himself, grinning at the smirk Violet gave. He forced a serious expression back onto his face. "That Gerald Ark guy he hangs out with on Earth. He's no good. He brainwashes him."

"Maybe they brainwash each other," Pida said and snickered.

"C'mon, I'm serious. Ark is an extraterrestrial. He promotes bad things on Earth."

Violet continued to eat silently, watching the two go back and forth in their conversation. She didn't want to believe any of it.

"Why would he be working with Russ? Do they wanna take over the world?"

"Ark's rap sheet is as long as his. And I bet his Uncle Rent is in it too."

"No way," Violet said. "Rent's sweet. He couldn't be part of whatever evil business that you're talking about."

"They're being forced to shut Ember Dice down. Without the game, Vi, I don't think that any of the pawns want us or them to survive."

"What are we supposed to do then?" Pida asked.

"We play like we always have. Normal. Keep the normalcy. We just have to get back to Earth alive."

"I still think you're being paranoid, Rivet. You're also showing way too much interest in Violet."

"Give me a break, Pida. I care about all of us up here. I don't want anyone to die in space."

"You're scared," Pida said. She took a long sip of coffee and looked right at Violet. "He's scared of the final battle."

"Am not. I just don't want to end up floating without a helmet in the vacuum."

"We'll be fine," Violet said, forcing a smile. "I have no idea how it's gonna end here, but at least your conversations make me feel less weird."

"Eccentric.  Eccentric is the word."  Rivet traded high-fives with Pida.

# 13

# The Wall

RUSSELL

There were two sides to each story, and in the end of the game, Russ knew his version of the truth would save his life. Violet seemed more interested in the other side of the story, always seeking answers to questions that had no place in Ember Dice. She had found the wall of Shield photos tucked down the sleep room corridor. She stared at it, using her precious recreation time to mourn the deaths of strangers.

"Accidents," Russ said, slowly wrapping his arms around Violet and kissing her neck from behind. He felt her lean into him, her body quivering.

"Were they all lost because of you?" she asked.

"I never wanted to lose my Shields." He put his mouth against her ear. "I just wanted to win."

"They were terrible at the game?"

"No." Russ looked back up at the photos. So many beautiful girls. "There were a few gems who fought well next to me. And I can say for certain, Cricket," he lowered his voice into a raspy whisper, "you are one of those gems."

"I'm happy I've done you proud," Violet said. She started to pull away, and he squeezed her tighter. "Russ, let me go now."

"Don't let me down, baby girl," Russ said. He shoved her out of his arms and whirled around to walk back toward the mess hall. He knew she was staring, watching him, as she trembled in absolute fear.

"This is my game," he said. "Mine."


VIOLET

The next afternoon of virtual gaming proved to be a lighthearted one, despite the strange encounter with Russ the evening before. Violet tried to keep his eerie words to herself as she nailed the Sky War level.

"Invert! Invert, babe!" Russ shouted.

"I am, Russ! Shoot him before he shoots me!"

"Increase speed, c'mon!"

"Shut up, Russell! I can fly this plane. Watch my back."

"You're lucky I let you be the pilot in this round. The Shields almost never get to head the flight."

Violet took off her headset for a break, smoothing her greasy long curls. "I love being the pilot."

"Not bad," Russ said. "Did you fly planes for real on Earth?"

"Nope. Just gotten good with the controls."

"Well done, babe. Well done, indeed."

She saw him roll his eyes as they resumed the level. "What'd I say?"

"Nothing. You're fantastic."

# 14

# Sciorlla

VIOLET

Time in Sciorlla flew every week, and despite the unpredictable moments of Russ trying to sabotage her mind and body, Violet was relieved to still be in the game by the start of the sixth and final month. She had worked obediently as a team with Russ and felt she was now due for a personal reward. Three other couples had gone home after publicly announcing their engagements, proving to be a grand and loving gesture, encouraged by the commanders, before the last days of Ember Dice. The rest of the Warriors and Shields remained in the daily routine, continuing to do the morning physical training and virtual game Bullet Rain.

COMMANDER RENT

During dinner in the mess hall on the night before the real battle, Rent announced the five couples who would be participating in the final honor of Ember Dice. Piper and Wesson flanked him as he stood tall and stiff, reading loudly from his tablet.

"The finalist couples are Warrior Igneous and Shield Peaches, Warrior Rivet and Shield Aura, Warrior Shred and Shield Pida,

Warrior Tuff and Shield Glory, and Warrior Russ and Shield Violet. Listen to me, each of you. The meeting concerning the real world battle will be held right after dinner. You will come aboard the Zippermare and there I will review what will occur between now and the last day on Sciorlla."

RUSSELL

"You may carry whatever weapon you like into battle," Rent said during the meeting. "Armor is not required but it is encouraged. Medical treatment is available at the announcement of the last team standing. Warriors, if your Shield is brought down and shouts a surrender, you must still fight. Shields, if your Warrior goes down in the same manner, you must keep fighting. Remember that kill shots are not allowed. You will endure physical injury in defending your partner, but the ultimate reward is the ownership of the Zippermare ship and an official wedding ceremony on Earth sponsored by Ember Dice, not to mention a last minute prize of a homestead of your choice."

"You're gonna give us a house?"

"That's correct, Igneous."

"How did you make it this far, man?" Russ asked him. "You've been the slowest of the Warrior pack."

Igneous shrugged and smiled. "My poetic charm brings me luck."

"It's gonna bring you broken ribs," Russ said with a scowl. "I'd avoid me and Vi on the field."

"Yeah, you're crazy. I know that."

"I'm more than crazy. I'm invincible."

VIOLET

There were two tents set up outside the Ember D base that

night. Shields slept in one, Warriors slept in the other. It was a privilege to sleep outside on another planet and Violet wanted to soak in each hour she could under the Sciorllan stars. There was no kiss goodnight from Russ, no flirting between couples. It was a quick and solemn walk from the Zippermare out onto the ground toward the tents.

"Dawn will come quick," Rent had told them. "For some of you, the battle tomorrow will go by in a blur, for others it will be a painful nightmare."

"Just survive," Violet said to herself as she settled in her sleeping bag.

The four other Shields snored around her as she lay awake thinking, planning, imagining the consequences of a life on Earth bound to Russell Watke. If it had been worth it on the first day, it should be worth it now. It should be worth it.

# 15

# Game Over

COMMANDER RENT

"This is it, gentlemen. All we can do is watch from here."

Rent, Piper, and Wesson stood at the panoramic window in the Zippermare, eyeing the sunrise and the tents set up near the designated battlefield.

"Headsets," Rent said.

They all put them on.

"Can they hear us?" Wesson asked.

"No. Not a word. This last fight is about one thing. Survival, no matter the cost. No help outside of your own team."

"A spectacular show, as always," Piper said, keeping his eyes on the window as he dipped his hand into a container of popcorn.

"Did you take that from the microwave?" Wesson asked with wide eyes.

"I did."

"That was mine."

Piper rolled his eyes at Wesson who dug into his pants pocket for his own snack. "Whatever. I have popcorn-flavored gum."

"You are so weird, kid."

VIOLET

She stepped out of the Shield tent in her battle outfit, gaining nods of respect from the other girls who had all discussed their strategies and armor ideas the previous night. Even Aura, the outlandish flirty cheater in Russell's secret fan club, kept from smirking or giggling amidst the serious tone of the morning. This was a real battle with real injuries to come and none of the Shields planned on swinging soft.

"Vi, wait up!"

Violet paused to look over her shoulder at Rivet jogging toward her. "Why do you keep talking to me?"

"I got your back, girl. Russ isn't killing any more Shields."

"I appreciate that, Rivet, but you don't have to follow me. Aura is your Shield. You need her."

"You and I both know she has cheated on me. And Russ..." Rivet glanced down. "He's been alone with her plenty of times."

Violet felt her face redden. Her chest tightened as she tried not to picture Russ and Aura together. "You're not very good with a rifle," she said to distract herself from the image. "Why'd you pick it?"

Rivet grinned as he held the long gun against his shoulder. He waited for her to smile back. "Ah, well, trying something different. Last time I used a crossbow and it broke within ten minutes. A Shield chucked a cannonball straight at me as I was aiming it."

"Cannonball?"

"Any weapon is permitted. It gets messy out there, Vi." He touched her shoulder. "Keep your head swiveling and your eyes open."

"I'll do my best, Rivet." Violet nodded and walked toward the

Warrior tent.

"Where you going?"

"Talk to Russ."

"After what I just told you? He's a cheating womanizer."

"Rivet," Violet said, "I already know that. But wouldn't it be appropriate for a Shield to have one last intimate chat with her Warrior before she protects his arrogant ass in war?"

"No shame in a last hurrah," Rivet said with a shrug. "Just be careful. I'll see you out there."

"See you, Warrior." Violet gave a flamboyant wave as she walked away from him.

"By the way," Rivet shouted behind her, "your outfit is adorable!"

Russ proved to be an absolute jerk in the smirk he gave as Violet entered the tent. "Who picked out your clothes?"

"You want me to run out there in a glittery manicure and fuchsia lipstick instead?"

He looked her up and down as he zipped up his hoodie and bent to tie the laces of his combat boots. "Let me think, Cricket. Sunglasses, t-shirt, faded jeans, frizzy hair, zero make-up, no armor, and a little handgun. I trust you will defend me just like that?"

"I'm solid with a pistol."

Russ scoffed as he put a piece of gum in his mouth. "Babe, you and I are screwed unless you change up that attire."

"I can win this with you, Russ. But I have one more question before we get this insanity over with."

"All right, Cricket. Shoot."

"How does this count as a battle if there are only five couples left? It'll be over in like twenty minutes if we all hit each other with bullets."

"It's not that simple."  Russ stood at one of the mirrors propped against the tent canvas and flicked cologne onto his neck and wrists.  "More will come from other planets. Outer planet participants. They are the ones who represent the CPU players in the virtual game. You won't see their faces, but there will be at least two hundred out there to add to the fantastic mayhem."

"A free-for-all," Violet said.

"Sure." Russ half-smiled. "Free-for-all."

"What weapon are you using?"

"It's a secret. Just keep running in front of me, Cricket, and I'll see you at the end."

His words sounded sweet and playful, but the wink he gave her as he swaggered out of the tent made her pulse pound.

"Head down," Violet told herself. "Just keep your head down."


RUSSELL

It would be over before it began.  That was the truth.  Russ twitched as he went forward, wearing the most basic of outfits, mind swirling with the hour yet to come. No one knew what was coming. None of them suspected it.

"Russ, how'd you sleep?  You ready to kick butt out there?" Rivet smiled as he stepped in line with him, watching the concentration on his face. "You good?"

"Never better."

"Where's your weapon?"

"Don't worry about it, bro. Fight your own battle."

"What are you doing? Why aren't you holding the broadsword from last time? No rifle? Where is it?"

"Shut up, Rivet. Let me do this."

"Do what?" Rivet's childish smile faded as he noticed Russ

fiddle with something in the pocket of his cargo pants. "Russ, please." He leaned in close, breathing the words into his ear. "Don't be stupid."

Russ backed away from him, grinning.

"Don't kill Violet," Rivet called out. "Don't you dare kill that Shield."


VIOLET

She stood in front of Russ, looking from right to left. Pida, Aura, Glory, and Peaches were all in front of their Warriors, poised to run. It was silent on the field.

"Where are the others?" Violet whispered.

"They're coming." Pida dropped to one knee. "Remember that none of us are on the same team."

"I'll try to go easy on ya," Aura said, sending a wave and wink down the line.

"No promises," Tuff said. "It's gonna be rough."

"Vi," Russ whispered into her ear, "when the signal sounds, sprint as fast as you can ahead of me. Clear the path and I'll have you back on Earth in no time. You and I get that house and the perfect wedding."

"No problem, Russ. I got this." Violet felt giddy as the massive outer planet army approached from the other end of the field. All the participants from that side were covered in suits and helmets.

"Run. Run, Violet."

"What?"

Rivet called out to her above the sound of the battle signal. "Run from Russ. Run, Violet!"

The five couples burst forward, Violet sprinting, pistol in hand. She didn't look back once. When she was struck by a bullet, it came from behind, and the pain didn't stop.  It kept coming. Rivet was yelling. Tuff was yelling.

"Russell, what are you doing? What the heck are you doing?"

# 16

# Detonation

COMMANDER RENT

"No! Don't shoot Russ! Don't shoot Russ!" Rent screamed as he watched Rivet running across the field with his rifle positioned to fire.

"They can't hear you," Wesson called to him as he tore off his headset.

"Land the ship and open the doors."

"Rent, get down!" Piper yelled. He ran after him, both of them ramming themselves into the doors.

"Land the ship, Wes! He's got a detonator!"

RIVET

The ticking of time froze in his mind as his eyes moved to Violet sprawled on the ground, crawling toward her pistol, to the bewildered faces of the Shields who still stood in defense of their Warriors. Russ appeared to be in a trance with one arm in the air, legs spread in a concrete stance of defiance against them all. Then he smiled at Rivet.

"Safe word," came his hoarse whisper.

Rivet's grip on the rifle slipped when he saw what Russ held above his head.

"No..." he mouthed.

The explosion knocked them out.


COMMANDER RENT

Carnage. Absolute carnage. Devastation. Murder on Sciorlla.

"What do we do, Commander?" Wesson hesitated walking through the field as dust continued to float in the air.

Piper looked around at the bodies, hands trembling as he pulled at his hair. "This is on us. Dammit, Rent. We let Russ do this."

"Gerald Ark helped him," Rent said as he walked through the debris. "He was not alone in this attack."

"Forget the extraterrestrial. We are all going to pay for Russell Watke's crimes!" Piper screamed.

"Find survivors. Come, Wes."

Wesson obeyed the somber Rent, fear replacing shock, as he sifted through the mess on the field.

"Violet's alive!" Piper lifted her into his arms minutes after his excited declaration.

* * *

"Where do we take them, Commander?"

Rent stared out at the deep space, feeling an anxious energy fill the Zippermare. His ship was a carrier of death and a catalyst for bloodshed. Their fate no longer belonged to Earth.

"Galaxy XA4300." He glanced down at Wesson who sat ready at the controls. "Erase everything."

Wesson nodded silently and prepped for the new coordinates.

"Violet Acklin, Rivet Dalrin, Pida Frake, Igneous Evans." Commander Rent spoke the names of the survivors while looking back toward where their battered bodies lay under blankets. He listened to their shallow breathing as he said, "welcome aboard."

*Peace out, Earth. These Warriors, these Shields, are mine. This war is not over. It has just begun.*

# About the Author

Han M. Greenbarg has been in love with writing fiction since childhood. She is an avid coffee drinker, proud dog mom, and lover of country music and war movies. She achieves her biggest jolts of inspiration while being out in nature, and especially enjoys crafting parallel worlds and post-apocalyptic settings.

**You can connect with me on:**

🌐 https://www.hanmgreenbarg.com

# Also by Han M Greenbarg

**Scurts Flightplan**
With three months left to live in a stifling, post-nuclear city, Damon Scurto believes he has one last shot at finding the grave of the woman who got away. He is best friends with a guy who eats paper, best frenemies with a convicted killer, and is the bane of his wine-drunk therapist's existence.